Tethers

Kimberly Kinnaman

ISBN: 979-8-9901496-2-5 (paperback)

ISBN: 979-8-9901496-3-2 (e-book)

ISBN: 979-8-9901496-4-9 (audiobook)

Library of Congress Control Number: 2024907005

This book is a work of fiction. All references to names, historical events, characters, beliefs, organizations, incidents, and places are products of the author's imagination or are used fictitiously.

Cover & Book Design by Kimberly Kinnaman

Printed by Kimberly Kinnaman Portland OR, United States of America

First printing edition, 2024

Dedication

To all the dreamers out there who were afraid of letting go, and decided to do it anyway.

Floating Away

Everything is connected. If you don't believe me, sit for just a moment, think about the things that you are connected to. Things that give your life meaning and tell you where you belong in this world.

Your family...

...your friends...

...your animals...

...your favorite recipe...

...the bartender that pours that whisky sour just right...

...your favorite barista because they know even though you're on a diet, you like that extra pump of flavor that you don't count the calories in...

...your favorite book...

...movie...

...tv show?

All these things tie you to this world...

...the big...

...and the little...

...they lend meaning to your life. *These* are the things worth living for. What would you do if you lost *all* of these things?

What would you have left to live for?

I can't remember the first time my feet left the ground, only the feeling of floating. At first, I was hovering only a few inches, still able to stretch my toes down and feel the ground beneath my feet. It was a fun sensation...

...weightlessness...

...I felt...

...free.

I could move around less restricted than ever before! Then one day, I stretched my toes out and realized, the ground was no longer within my reach. That freedom turned to fire in the pit of my stomach. Panic crept from my outstretched toes up through my spine, to the tip of my head.

Realization gripping me...

...once you get high enough...

...you almost never come back down...

Making connections from the air is nearly impossible.

They're called tethers, these things that tie us to the world. You can't see them...

...you *feel* them.

Each one has its own weight, texture, and durability.

Some are stronger than others...

...the bond between lovers.

Some are temporary...

...the acquaintance you see in the elevator on the way up to work each day.

Some people hold onto theirs for a lifetime...

...the bond between a parent and a child.

If you have too many they become unbearably heavy, rooting you to the spot until you're ready to let some of them go. Too few has the opposite effect, you start to drift away, upward, where there are no more tethers to be forged.

It is a delicate balance to have enough without too many, and to know when to pick up more and when to put some down.

Some people will nearly kill themselves...

...not wanting to let go.

Others...

...may achieve that feat.

Very few handle their tethers flawlessly, becoming the envy of their communities. No burden too heavy, no tether too restraining, they glide through life as if they're unaffected by the tethers they carry.

Balance...

...the ultimate goal of all...

...the reality of so few...

I've never wished more than I do in this moment that I knew their secret. How do they balance everything and keep their feet on the ground without being too weighed down?

How do they manage life?

Because mine...

...is slipping away from me...

...inch...

...by inch...

...and I don't know how...

...to get my feet back on solid ground.

One Foot off the Ground

I'm hovering a foot from the ground, at least I think I'm a foot from the ground. Although, there is no accurate way for me to measure how far I've drifted away. I could use the measuring app on my phone, but I don't believe it would be accurate, and I should save the battery (85%) in case of emergency. You would think floating away is an emergency, but there you would be wrong, this is just another Tuesday.

I'm beginning to wonder if I want to set foot back on the ground. I've forgotten what it felt like to have a solid feeling beneath my feet.

What if I keep floating?

How high until the air thins and I suffocate?

"Hello?" I've been calling out to everyone passing by. "Can you spare a second? Can you spare an ear?"

Have I become invisible since my feet left the ground?

"CAN'T YOU SEE ME? DON'T YOU CARE? I DON'T KNOW WHAT ELSE TO DO! SOMEBODY... Please! Talk to me."

It was no use; people don't talk to floaters. You spend your entire life holding onto the most important tethers and learning to let go of everything and everyone else. Bearing the burden of your own connections is more than enough for anyone, adding another you don't need is nearly impossible.

"Please!? Someone.... *Anyone?*"

Why do I keep trying? People won't even look at me. Soon enough they won't have to, once I hit the clouds no one will have the burden of seeing me drift away.

Out of sight.

Out of mind.

Nothing left to hold me down.

Nothing...

...keeping me connected to the ground.

Two Feet off the Ground

Melancholy. I cannot think of another word to describe the impending doom of this slow ascension into oblivion. Close enough to the ground that it makes no sense that I cannot touch it.

It's right there!

It's *just* out of my reach, if only I could stretch out!

If I could convince someone to give me an anchor point! I *may* be able to stay.

I don't have to float away.

If someone would just *listen*...

...when I scream.

If anyone would

just

help

me

stay!

I want to stay!

I don't want to float away!

I wonder if floating is like flying.

I'm not the only one who can't seem to forge new tethers, every so often someone floats away.

What happens to them?

Let's try...

...focus all our effort on...

...swimming, in the sky?

I just look silly. I never learned to swim. I end up doing a frog stroke that isn't getting me anywhere. I did make someone laugh though, but soon as I looked in their direction they ran away. Too bad I can't follow anyone and *make* them listen.

At least I know I'm not invisible.

I think I'll take advantage of this zero-gravity thing and take a nap. Since those who pass by act as though they cannot see me, I doubt that they'll worry about hearing me snore. They probably much prefer it to my screaming.

This might be one of the best perks to being forgotten...

...you sleep like a baby.

Sometimes that means screaming and crying through the night; sometimes it means you wake up without that pesky crick in the neck that a stiff mattress and wrong size pillow provide.

Maybe floating away isn't so bad after all...

...at least...

...not at this height.

Three Feet off the Ground

O pening your eyes to the lack of a blanket over your head is jarring.

Is this really happening?

This is really happening, like this is *really* my reality. This is, this is really happening; this is really happening. This... maybe I should shut my eyes again and this will all go away. I must have woken up from one bad dream into another! There's no way that I'm *actually* floating away.

No.

No way.

Eyes pressed tightly together I shake my head, refusing to believe this is real.

This can't be real, no way this is real.

I don't want to open them again, the lack of solidity around me confirms that when I do...

...I will still be living this nightmare.

If I open them again the tears will start to flow again.

If I open them again...

...this is real...

This is real.

I lost another tether today...

...my favorite book.

I can't get to it, I can't pick it up and read it and smell that old book smell, stroking the spine as I flop it open onto my lap to read for the millionth time.

I'm not even sure that I want to read it again.

I know the story by heart, boy meets girl, boy insults girl, boy falls in love with girl, girl rejects boy (as she should), boy makes grand gesture of his love for her and they live...

...happily...ever...after...

Maybe if I had spent less time with my nose in that book and more time interacting with others, I wouldn't be floating into oblivion. Maybe I should try flying again...

...I think I can doggy paddle.

Four Feet off the Ground

I did interact with others. I fell in love, I found friendships, I worked at a job I loved, I had family. I had so many tethers that it was hard to move.

I was managing, I was going to get married. We were planning, going to marriage counseling and the topic of kids came up. I didn't want to have a baby...

...a baby is a heavy burden to bear...

When you're born, you are connected to so many things, and the closest tether in this world is your mother. She carries you around with the weight of the world literally attached, hundreds of tethers to navigate.

Having babies isn't for the faint of heart.

You must have the strength to share the load, a mother alone would be tied to the spot, unable to move. Without a community, the pair would starve, the mother unable to let go of her baby and the baby unable to sever the ties that bind them to this world so tightly. I was already having a hard time moving around and to have an infant... I wouldn't be able to move unless I gave up many of my own tethers.

I relented.

I loved him.

He loved me.

We would navigate this together. We can do this! I started to sever some of my tethers leading up to our big day and our new family together.

Hobbies, arts and crafts, hiking, singing...

...all the little things that brought so much joy into my life but also carried a tie that weighed me down.

I started to give them up.

Driving, and my car... I didn't need these, he could drive me to appointments.

My apartment, I didn't need it anymore, we moved me into his house. I didn't have a lot to move, my favorite book, and some odd kitchen utensils. When everything you own ties you down, you tend to not own a lot. By this time, I was feeling much better about our future together. As I lost many of my own tethers and started to rely on him, our tether strengthened becoming my strongest tie to this life. I still had my family and friends tying me to the ground, but a lot of the weight I was carrying was gone.

The relief was amazing.

I *almost* didn't miss any of the tethers that I had given up.

My dress was huge, with all the tethers broken I could stand the extra weight. When I started down that isle, I felt like the world was perfect....

> ...*my world* was perfect....

...then I looked up to the place where my groom should have been, and he wasn't there.

> I took a step closer, searching the alter for him...

> ...maybe he was late...

> ...I looked out over the crowd...

> ...then I felt it...

The tether that had tied us together was ripping from my chest, taking a piece of my heart with it.

Everyone knew instantly, as a blood curdling scream left my lips, I collapsed in the isle unable to move. My friends picked me up and took me to my parent's house, cleaned me up and put me to bed.

Do you ever get back out of bed when you've suffered a broken heart?

> You have to.

> Life keeps on moving, even when you don't.

Your body will continue to function even as you feel your chest cavity fill from the hole in your heart, making every breath unbearably hard. The pressure eventually acts as a tourniquet for the muscle, allowing it to repair itself...

...mostly.

What are the options, become a burden to those around you, lost in your sorrow, drowning in a pillow of your own tears? Threatening their lives as they're dragged down by the tether connecting you. Someone has to let go, you have to keep trying, or you'll lose everyone around you, not just yourself.

As long as you keep struggling through each breath...

...you will recover...

...eventually.

When I was able to recover...

...I found that my feet no longer touched the ground.

Five Feet off the Ground

Swimming's getting me nowhere. You can't swim through the air; gaseous molecules aren't dense enough to provide traction.

I was a scientist once

I worked in a lab discovering the best chemical compounds to make your whites whiter while not leaving behind a stinky chemical smell. I remember laughing in the bathroom at the end of each day at the marks left on my face from my goggles. Protective wear always a requirement because chemical fumes are no joke. My coworkers were some of my best friends. We went to school together; we each worked hard to share the academic load and keep each other on track. When we got jobs at the same company we were elated. After work drinks at Franklins Pub downtown were the best way to start a weekend.

I haven't seen that pub in years,

                              I wonder if it's still open.

I haven't seen any of those friends in years,

                        I wonder if any of them have floated away?

Wouldn't it be crazy to run into someone I knew up here in the sky. How strange that losing some tethers will nearly kill you while others you don't even notice slip away.

I keep all these memories on my phone, pictures of the good times, and the bad, to remind me of how much life I have lived and how much life I have to look forward to.

...Right now...

...it's serving as a reminder of everything I lost the moment I let my feet leave the ground.

Nostalgia...

...is a bitch...

I put my phone back in my pocket (57%)

Ten Feet off the Ground

I can spin in the air like a top. There's really nothing else to do now, just spin in circles until I get sick. I don't have to worry about cleaning up after myself if I retch because...

...I can't reach the ground.

I drift this way and that with the gusts of wind, I'm trying to aim for a tree. If I can get ahold of the branches maybe I can anchor myself to the spot.

I don't know if I want to keep floating up...

...it's cold...

...just hanging around in the air.

I also don't know if I really want to come back down...

...there's nothing left for me on the ground.

Twenty Feet off the Ground

I 've lost track of how long I've been floating, minutes, hours, days, weeks? I'm honestly surprised that I've made it this high.

I wonder how high I'll float.

I wonder how people eat up here. Maybe I'll starve to death, that shouldn't be a comforting thought but...

...it is.

I haven't felt hunger since I started floating away, probably a good thing because I have yet to see a floating porta potty. I haven't even thought about food.

What was the last thing that I ate?

Did I have a favorite food?

Why can't I remember these things?

My mouth moves to mimic eating, but I can't remember the textures or tastes of food. My tongue swipes across my lips, hoping to wet the chapped feeling, but it serves more as sandpaper reminding me that I have not had a drink since floating either.

The irony isn't lost on me, that I have lost so many tethers that I am floating away, and the mere act of floating has severed all tethers to sustenance.

Maybe once you're sky high you don't need it anymore? That might be too optimistic for this situation...

Oh well...

...maybe I'm right...

...there's no one here to disagree with me.

What do you call optimism in the face of destruction?

I think that's called hope.

What exactly I'm hoping for, I am uncertain of at this height, but at least I haven't given up...

...yet.

Forty Feet off the Ground

I lost another tether today, I felt it slip from my heart, it didn't rip my heart into pieces like my would-be wedding day.

I can feel tears soak into my shirt as I press my eyes trying to stop the damage before it's too late.

It was subtle, a tether that has been wrapped around my heart my entire life, one that I have been allowing to weaken over time, allowing it to leave without taking too much of my heart for my body to bare.

It'll leave a scar...

...a memory that I will never lose...

...no matter how high I drift.

I can't tell who I lost, my mother or father, but I know it's one of them. I don't think anyone will be able to find me to tell me the news. I'm far from where I started floating away.

I can't stop these tears...

...not yet...

...I don't think I'm supposed to.

When you lose someone so important to you, more than just walking away; the permanence of death reopens old wounds. Even if you've already grieved the loss of that person, it's only natural to grieve them all over again. It's supposed to hurt, the pain teaches us a lesson...

...that life and love are temporary...

...but that the feelings of living and loving...

...are worth the pain.

I guess the luck of being this high is that I no longer have to worry about drifting into traffic.

I started letting go of the tethers to my parents after my failed attempt at the altar, they took care of me the best they could while I recovered but it was a huge burden and it weighed them down more than they needed.

I had to start letting go...

...to save them.

Their bodies cannot bare the extra weight; as you age you can carry less and less. It was the best thing I could do for them...

...walking away...

...even if it was the worst choice for myself.

I wonder what happens when you pass away, death being the knife that severs all tethers in a single swipe.

Do lifeless bodies float?

If they do how come the sky isn't full of corpses? Is this why we bury bodies, to keep them from filling the sky. Could you imagine, bodies floating into the atmosphere and burning to a crisp; I wonder if every time you see a shooting star it's a corpse burning through the atmosphere.

Maybe this isn't what I should be thinking, about losing a parent, but the thoughts are my only company.

I might be joining them soon...

...at least there's comfort in that thought.

The tears slow gradually, but I don't believe they will end anytime soon. My body convulses, shivering violently as the wind catches my damp t-shirt. The chatter of my teeth is likely audible for miles in all directions, those below could use the sound as a homing beacon to find me, not that anyone's looking.

Maybe...

...if I learned not to cry...

...I wouldn't have to suffer through the cold.

The chills wracking my body remind me of the damage loss can trigger.

Body...

...and...

...soul...

Eighty Feet off the Ground

I 've never had to think about whether I was scared of heights until this impromptu trip to the sky. I guess this is different, the traditional fear of heights is really about falling, not so much the heights themselves. I don't believe I will be falling because I keep moving upward.

I wonder exactly how high I am now.

The cars look like toys, when I get bored (let's face it I'm always bored) I pretend that I'm driving them along the roads down there; I hold the fate of those vehicles in my hands.

Muahahaha.... if I wanted, I could just spin them out of control and watch them scream!

Oh...

No...

I can't...

They aren't really in my hand...

...nothing, is in my hands...

...not even my own life anymore.

Everything feels so far out of my reach...

...so far out of my control...

What do I even have left?

I have *myself.*

I can hold *me.*

I can give *myself* a hug.

I have *me* in my hands.

One Hundred Feet off the Ground

Taking my fate back into my own hands. How can I do that? I keep floating and I can't get anywhere I want to go. Is there anywhere I want to go?

Just back down...

...back down to...

I'm not sure there *is* anything on the ground waiting for me. I suppose that's freeing, I could go anywhere.

Freedom...

...feels a lot like alone to me.

Alone...

...what a lonely word.

I guess I can try flying again, but even when I flap my arms like wings, I'm only fooling myself, and I'm high enough now that I can hear the birds laughing at me.

How does that children's game go?

Light as a feather, stiff as a board, and you float. I'm neither of those things and I'm floating. So, this might not work, but if I want to get down maybe I can reverse this spell?

Heavy as a brick...

...no that's not heavy enough.

Heavy as a boulder...

a car...

an elephant...

a building?

Yeah, heavy as a building, and the opposite of stiff, floppy as a...

...disk.

Floppy like a pancake. Yeah, I like that...

...or jiggly as jello.

I'm getting tired, curling into myself I chant...

"Heavy as a building, floppy as a pancake..."

"...Heavy as a building, jiggly as jello..."

"...Heavy..."

Until I can't anymore...

                                        ...and sleep overtakes me.

Two Hundred Feet off the Ground

The world looks so much more peaceful from up here. I can't see the litter on the ground...

...or smell the smokers...

...or the transients, although they can't really help the way they smell.

The view is sweeping landscapes at this height, the earth is stunningly beautiful. Maybe if I had had this view all along, things would be different. That old trope, if I knew then what I know now...

...maybe *that* is faulty thinking.

I didn't know then what I know now, and it's not that bad to float. I'm free-ish. I mean there's nothing really to enjoy here in the sky...

...just me...

I could use a glass of wine to go with this spectacular view. Or perhaps an entire bottle, that might take the edge off the height I'm currently seeing the world from.

I've seen a lot more animals, and I've stretched a lot trying to swim... and fly. The lack of weight holding me down has allowed my body to relax and for the first time in my life I feel, physically, ok.

But I'm scared.

What happens if I never come back down?

I guess that's where fear comes from...

...the unknown.

If I knew what fate awaited me would I still be scared?

I don't have much choice other than finding out, better make the best of the time between. Maybe I will find another floater up here and we could talk, you would think in a world of 8 billion people, I would've run into another by now... Am I?

No...

...I can't be the only one who's failed at living.

Three Hundred Feet off the Ground

I wish I felt courageous. I wish I felt like even though I'm scared, I'm doing this anyways...

...from choice.

But choice feels like an illusion as I continue to ascend.

What choice did I have but to float away?

What choice could've saved me from this fate?

What could I have tethered myself to that would be strong enough to keep me connected to the ground?

Is it too late?

Can I think of something that I still feel connected to?

I know I still have at least one tether...

...I can feel it.

The tether I have to my other parent is slipping away, I feel it growing thinner and weaker as I climb.

...It won't last much longer...

I take out my phone (2%) and look at photos of my parents, the pain of seeing us together and happy, feet planted firmly on solid ground...

...has my eyes leaking again...

"I can't keep doing this," I say to myself, and I guess my phone agrees, as the screen fades to black – a blinking – red – dead battery symbol - flashes across the screen – taunting me with the promise of life, if only...

...I could connect.

What use do I have of this device?

I watch it slip from my hands, the one thing that was reminding me of the life I have lived. All my memories, faded out like the blank screen, soon to be shattered on the ground.

Maybe I shouldn't have dropped that...

...I really hope it doesn't land on someone's head...

...oops.

Four Hundred Feet off the Ground

I 'm high enough that I can't make out individual people any-more. They're more like...

...floating specks...

...human blobs...

...unrecognizable...

If anyone is watching me, I can't tell. They could just as easily think that I'm a bird. A big...

...funny shaped bird...

...who has scrawny wings...

...that I keep trying to force to work for me, but they just aren't getting me anywhere.

I wonder if this is what a lost balloon feels like, if a lost balloon had feelings. Although, I think there would be something bittersweet about being a lost balloon. Slipping free from a loved one's hands, rising to its full potential as the one who lost it stays on the ground. Staring longingly...

...heartbroken by the loss...

The balloon would know it's worth, know it was loved, know it was missed. It would rise, proud, knowing it was being watched by the one who loved it until it became an imperceptible speck of color in the sky, barely discernable from the atmosphere.

I wish I knew someone was watching me...

...wishing I would come back to them...

...Hoping that I don't pop...

...that I reach my full potential...

...so they can swell with pride even though they lost me to the atmosphere.

No one is watching.

No one is waiting for my return.

No one seems to even notice that I'm gone...

...that I'm floating away.

That the danger of *popping* is so real, and I might prefer to pop over ever coming back down.

I wonder if heads explode like helium balloons...

...I hope not...

How high does a balloon get before it pops?

I wonder if I'll get to see one from up here, maybe it could become my companion.

Five Hundred Feet off the Ground

The closer I float to the clouds...

...the more I wonder if I will ever touch the ground again...

This thought always sparks the idea...

...that I might not want to.

One Thousand Feet off the Ground

A slow free fall in reverse, ascension into the heavens. I've finally reached the clouds. There is an inescapable emptiness within me. I feel as though I left my guts on the ground. A little less connected to everything down below.

A lot, less connected, to everything down below.

"BUT I TRIED!"

Fully enveloped in the feeling of weightlessness. It might have been better if I were falling...

...losing all of the air from my lungs...

...gasping as I hit the ground...

...at least then I could feel something...

...anything...

...but this...

...nothingness.

Condensation confuses my senses, I can feel cold wet streaks running down my face, but I'm unsure if I'm crying or if it's the clouds touching my face.

"I'VE DONE EVERYTHING RIGHT..."

...My voice cracks as I continue to scream out, faltering I sob...

"I've done everything right."

No amount of screaming or tears can stop me from rising higher into the clouds. My fingertips tracing the trails along my cheeks, at least it's a cloudy night...

...no one below will know these are tears falling from above...

I press my fingers into my eyes, a tourniquet for these tears, but nothing can stop them from flowing.

Nestling into a bed of clouds feels empty, they're not the soft fluffy pillows we imagine them to be. No. Clouds are dense collections of water droplets, perhaps if I float in them long enough, I can be the first person to drown in the sky.

No one will be able to see me cry myself to sleep, shivering as the clouds soak through my layers. My chest aches as sobs wrack my body, until I'm too exhausted to cry, and gentle sobs pull from my lungs as I fade into sleep.

You don't come back down to earth when you're dreaming, even if you can feel the soft blades of grass beneath your toes and hear the trickling of water in a nearby stream. These dreams are simply a tease because now you know, you are *never* going to touch that of which you dream.

I don't want to wake up, this is a cold reality.

I pass into and out of sleep, but it doesn't feel like I'm ascending any longer. It seems my last tether has been pulled taut, weakly hanging onto me as I float on the edge of oblivion.

Why am I still holding onto a life I no longer know how to live?

What is still tying me to the earth?

Memory?

Love?

Determination?

Stubbornness?

In
The
Clouds

M y voice is hoarse from all the useless screaming, I can't muster the energy to continue asking for help. No one can hear me from up here.

Not like anyone would care...

...I don't even care anymore.

Maybe this is better?

What was so great down there anyway?

I can't remember what my life looked like before this moment, it's almost as if floating has disconnected me from even the things that I held most dear.

There's a single tether left tying me to the life that I used to know. The life that is so far out of my reach that I cannot even see it anymore. I don't know what it is, but it has grown steadily stronger as all my other tethers have weakened and fallen away. It is the sole survivor of this flight, and I have a growing suspicion that it is one of my own making.

Not something that others have offered.

Not something that can be taken from me.

Something that just *is*.

Something that only *I* can let go of.

It isn't strong enough to bring me back down, it's barely tying me to the ground...

...but it's there...

...I can feel it...

...a whisper of hope as I continue to float through the clouds.

I have reached the *literal* end of my rope. I cannot ascend further without letting go, and there is no way back down. What do I do? What do I do.... I don't know what awaits beyond this cloud cover, I don't know what to expect, or if letting go is the end. But I do know that staying where I am is a dead end. Dead, meaning I would be dead if I stay here. If the options are death by fear and holding on, or death by adventure and letting go, perhaps it's time to take that leap of faith, that courageous step to learn what is awaiting me beyond the clouds.

God, I hope it's not dead bodies.

What if letting go is the death sentence, and staying put is survival? I haven't eaten or drank since my feet left the ground, maybe floating here is a preservation of sorts. As long as I stay here, I should survive. Letting go I have no idea what awaits me. I could float up into oblivion, I could suffocate, or burn to a crisp. I could *die*. I don't want to die, isn't that what this last tether is anyways, my connection to the ground, my will to stay.

What if I let go of my will to stay?

My will to live?

But what kind of life is floating in the clouds? The view is terrible and I'm freezing, soaked to the bone. A blanket of clouds doesn't know how to keep a body warm. We need to change our terminology, perhaps we could call them a puddle of clouds, or an ocean of clouds, a stream of clouds, a frigid cloud bank, or something more fitting like...

...impending doom.

Perhaps staying here is the death sentence after all. I might just freeze to death. Although, that might be better than burning to a crisp, I've heard that when you freeze you hallucinate and your end is happy, even if every moment leading up to that switch flipping in your brain is excruciatingly painful.

What if I let go and I suddenly plummet to my death? I have never felt every muscle in my body tense up so quickly. It's terrifying...

...and exhilarating!

I don't know what to expect. None of these options sound good, but at this point what do I have left to lose?

Only...

...my life.

Above The Clouds

I close my eyes, take one last deep breath, ripping this last tether from my soul as I exhale. My scream thunders through the sky, my body aches as an electrical storm passes through me, igniting every nerve ending.

Letting go was *always* the only real option.

Choice was an illusion that I was using to fool myself into a small semblance of comfort, when I had none. I don't know if I can open my eyes again, I may have spent all of my courage on that final act. It doesn't feel like I'm falling, but what does falling feel like? That amusement park ride, where the wind meets your face, stealing the air from your lungs until you're frightened that you may never take another breath? Or the feeling of first love, looking into the eyes of the person you know you want to spend eternity - at least, the fraction you get of eternity - with. Stomach left behind, body plummeting down, lungs tight, the shallowest breath keeping you from blacking out, living the thrill of riding on the edge of oblivion, ready to meet the earth one final time.

No...

...this doesn't feel like falling...

...but that doesn't mean I'm safe.

How do you open your eyes when you don't know what you expect to see? You can't know. You've never lived through this before. Has anyone? People sometimes float away, but where do they go? No one talks about it which leads me to believe either they don't know...

                              ...or it's too sad to talk about.

Am I going to die?

Am I already dead?

Frozen, that's the feeling, cold, alone, muscles tight. They feel entirely out of my control. What's new, nothing has been *in* my control for quite some time. Nothing has ever been in my control. Nothing but me. I haven't moved. That is a choice, and I think it's time to start making a new one.

Count down...

Three... Deep breath in, slow exhale.

Two... Relax my face, even if the rest of my body won't listen, I need to know what I'm facing.

One... Slowly, *calm* I whisper to myself, I pry one eye open at a time.

I'm still suspended in the air, afloat, untethered to the ground below, but the sky above isn't calling me home. I'm not moving...

I'm not moving!

...I'm...

...not...

...moving...

Am I stuck? *Can* I move? Should I try swimming again? No one can see me, couldn't hurt! Deep breath in, what if moving drops me? Oh well, too late. I try to relax my muscles; they refuse to move. Fear has me in a choke hold.

Deep breath in.

And another.

And another.

It's ok, it's ok. It will be ok, either way, no matter what happens, this is the *end of this ride*. I won't suffer anymore. I convince my arms to release.

As I swing them upward, I rise, breaking through the top of the cloud cover. *Gasp* My lungs pull in more air than they have held in longer than I can remember. An ocean of clouds was fitting. All I see are clouds stretching on for eternity in all directions. An eternity that I am so happy to be a part of. The sun is setting, giving the illusion of being safe and sound on a beach, watching one of life's most beautiful scenes.

I'm not dead.

Tears of joy streak down my face and I have never felt more relieved to find myself alive.

But how?

For the first time since floating, I don't feel weightless, I don't feel scared. A heaviness surrounds me, an all-consuming feeling of support, like something is holding me in the air, no longer pulling me in any direction against my will. Cocking my head to look over my shoulder I see nothing, but I can feel a weight that I didn't have before. A solidness arising from my soul, a wholeness that has driven the imponderous feeling away. I reach up, touching what feels like tethers, intwined, tangled within each other tightly, swaying in the breeze, fluttering, keeping me afloat.

Could it be?

Remnants of the life I used to live, tethers that have broken, leaving behind hanging threads invisible to the eye but felt with the soul. That these remnants of my severed tethers have become.... *wings?* I wouldn't believe it if I couldn't touch them myself.

...I...

...have...

...wings...

Invisible, but all my own. Every heartbreak, every pain, every failure.

Each – severed – tether left behind a fragment that I thought I would carry for eternity and now they will carry me. A long and heavy sigh of relief, my soul is settled in this moment. I feel, ready, to meet any fate along this journey. Surviving has given me freedom, real freedom, wings, a choice I didn't think I would ever have again.

I can return...

...I can keep flying...

...I can soar...

There are no more limits, no need of fear.

I.

Am.

Free.

About the Author

K imberly Kinnaman (Kiki) is an indie author located in the Pacific Northwest. She spends her time reading, writing, singing, and enjoying life with her two kids. She is a couch potato who dreams of an outdoor lifestyle, and spends most afternoons lost in some existential abyss. She has a BS in Science from Portland State University, but has taken time away from academia in the pursuit of happiness. If you were to ask her what her most prized possession in this world was, she would tell you it was her best friend.

Love you Stephanie!